The Fabulous Mr Frank & the Cupcake Catastrophe

written & illustrated by Kate Ainsworth

edited by E. Rachael Hardcastle

CW00860060

ISBN: 978-1-7399188-1-1

Edited by E. Rachael Hardcastle
Formatted by E. Rachael Hardcastle
Written by Kate Ainsworth
Illustrated by Kate Ainsworth

Published by Curious Cat Books, United Kingdom
For further information contact www.curiouscatbooks.co.uk

First Edition

Poppy and Harvey's birthdays were coming soon,
and their party was booked in a gigantic room.
There'd be magic and music and sweeties galore,
plus prizes, surprises and presents in store.

For days Mum was baking with eggs and with flour,
to make the most scrumptious cupcake tower.

On the table they sat, being eyed by someone;
a doggy called Frank wanted them all in his tum!

Frank's eyes were like saucers,
so round and so big!
No wonder his family
called him Bat Pig.

Up went Frank's paws, the plates clattered and CRASHED!

WHEEEEE went the cakes, tumbling down with a SMASH!

They heard the commotion, and rushed in the room.
The smiles on their faces soon turned to doom.

They started to whimper,
a tear in their eye,
"Our cakes, our cakes!"
they shrieked and
they cried.

They wept on the sofa, then ran through the door.
They wept in the garden, and wept on the floor.

"Stop!" shouted Mummy. "I know it's a shame,
but you know how Mr Frank loves to play games."

"Hop in the car, the cakes will have to wait,
Don't forget, we've got a party room to decorate!"

Meanwhile, in the house,
while Frank was alone,
he got straight to work,
picking up the 'bone phone'.

He phoned all his friends, like Super Sausage Sid,

Betsie the Bichon and a Chihuahua called Kid.

No one would've guessed that these four pups,
could divide out flour into measuring cups.
But measure they did, and scoop, mix and bake,
until they had made 20 more cupcakes!

They iced them, displayed them,
with love and with care,
(carefully picking off any stray hairs).

"Goodbye," Frank said,
"you're all wonderful mates."
And as they trotted out,
the car rolled through the gates.

"We're home!" called Poppy, "and ready for party fun."
Little did they know, just what Frank had done.

A proud looking Frank sat by his creation,
"Did you make these?" Frank nods in affirmation.

"Wow!" shout the kids,
"You've just saved the day!"
In the most Fabulous Mr Frank way.

The many names of Mr Frank:

Author's Note

For my wonderful children.

Thank you for choosing my book.
I hope you've enjoyed it.
God bless you all.
For more information about my other titles, please visit:
www.fabulousmrfrank.com

The Original Mr Frank →

Lightning Source UK Ltd.
Milton Keynes UK
UKRC041056180422
401669UK00001B/1